Bungalow Fungalow

Poems by Pegi Deitz Shea

Illustrated by Elizabeth Sayles

Clarion Books

NEW YORK

Clarion Books
a Houghton Mifflin Company imprint
215 Park Avenue South, New York, NY 10003
Text copyright © 1991 by Pegi Deitz Shea
Illustrations copyright © 1991 by Elizabeth Sayles

Library of Congress Cataloging-in-Publication Data
Shea, Pegi Deitz.
Bungalow fungalow / by Pegi Deitz Shea ; illustrated by Elizabeth
Sayles.
p. cm.
Summary: Fifteen poems celebrate the fun of a summer vacation at
the beach, through the eyes of a young boy.
ISBN 0-395-55387-3
1. Children's poetry, American.   2. Vacations—Juvenile poetry.
3. Seashore—Juvenile poetry.   [1. Vacations—Poetry.   2. Seashore—
Poetry.   3. American poetry.]   I. Sayles, Elizabeth, ill.
II. Title.
PS3539.H39123B86   1991   90-33333
811′.54—dc20   CIP
AC

WOZ 10 9 8 7 6 5 4 3 2 1

For Aunt Ann and Uncle Frank Toole,
whose bungalow was the first I learned to love.
—P.D.S.

To my brother Michael.
—E.S.

The Invitation

It's here, finally!
Stamps with waves on them.
Hmmmmm…ahhhhhh,
it even smells like the sea.

Whoa, look at this stuff:
shells, a gull feather,
a crab claw, and sand,
sand, even more sand.

And a letter to me, Billy Toole!

Dear Billy,
    Please come to Beach Haven
    and stay for a week.
    And if your mom and dad
    and Sport have been good,
    they can come, too.
        Love,
        Nana & Pop-Pop

P.S. Here's a little something
    to get you started
    on your first castle.

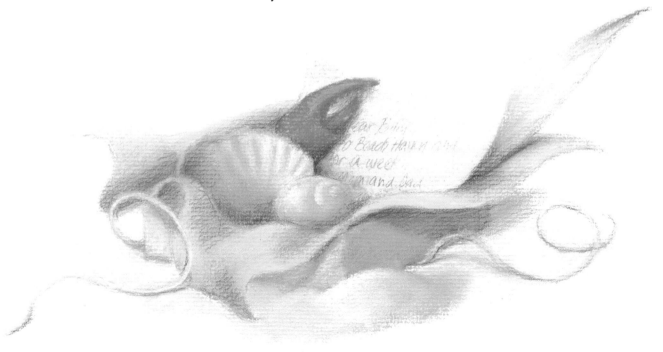

Packing Up

Here's my bathing suit.
Ugh. Ouch—too stiff,
too faded, too small.
Guess I need a new one.
I'm too big for little
green fishes anyway.

Hey, my flip flops!
Flip flop, flip flop,
flap, floop. Uh oh.
Need a new pair
to go with a new suit.
Could use some new shades, too.

My mask fits OK,
could use a scrubbin',
and my boats all float,
they don't need nothin'.

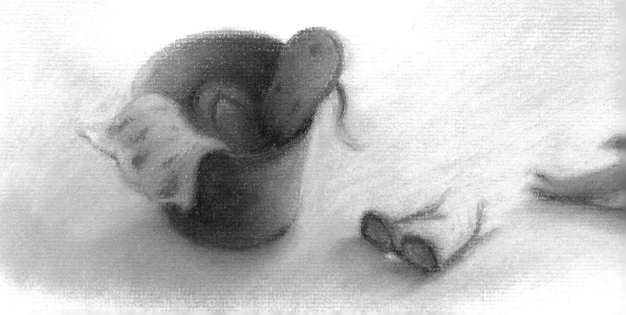

Sand conveyor belt works,
it's still a little gritty.
Pail and shovel are ready
to build a sand city.

I'll tunnel me a way out
of this hot sticky town,
all the way to the docks
of my own summer town.

7

Stuffed Station Wagon

Beach chairs stacked
on the roof of the car,
bicycles chained to the rack,
groceries crammed in between the seats,
suitcases jammed in the back.

Where am I going to sit?
Let me see, let me see.
If I jiggle this bag a bit,
and wriggle that box an inch,
I could squeeze in here, a perfect fit!

Well, almost.

Got an umbrella jabbing
me under my arm,
a beach blanket itching my lap,
piles of books crowding my feet
and Sportie nosing my hat.

Just go easy on the bumps,
OK, Dad?

The Ride to the Beach

When I was little,
I used to whine,
"Are we there yet?"
But now I know…

When the sun comes up
in front of our car,
we've only started.

When we cross the bridge
over New York Bay,
we're almost halfway.

When we drive through the Pinelands
and see the deer,
we're just about there.

When yards are yellow pebbles,
and cars make way for bikes,
when the sky goes on forever
and brown birds become white,

We're here.

Bungalow

Bun ga low. Bun galow.
(What a crazy word.)
Bungalow Donegalow.
Fungalow Gungalow,
Gunga Din!

Tarzan in the Jungalow
captures King Kongalow,
and the Flying Nungalow
goes for a Rungalow
while I play in the Sungalow!

Bun ga low.
Bun go high?
Bun go to the beach.

The First Thing

After kisses hello,
the first thing I do
is take off my shoes
and run on the dunes,

Down to the hard sand,
race waves up and back,
then flop in the surf,
get sand in my pants,

And climb on the jetty,
look out over the sea.
For one whole week
this belongs to me.

I Love
Nana & Pop-Pop's
Bungalow

The whole front yard
is one big sandbox,
and the backyard
goes down to the sea.

I shriek with sea gulls
on the fenceposts,
I flap with wet towels
in the wind,

Hide out for hours
in the outdoor shower,
watch the water disappear
through wood slats,

Track sand and dirt
through the kitchen,
leave round wet marks
on the couch.

I investigate ships
inside bottles,
listen for the sea
in a conch,

Put elbows on the table
during dinner,
throw the leftovers
to hovering birds,

After ice cream, beat Pop-Pop
at checkers,
help Mom move my cot
to the porch.

And there,
in my bed,
I can count
all the stars.
I can taste
and smell
salty air,

And listen
to the waves
roll onto the sand,
listen to the waves roll,
listen to the waves,
listen, waves,
listen, waves,
listen, waves, waves, waves.

Surf's Up Shop

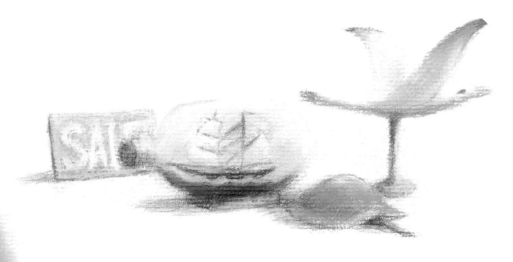

Mom takes me to Surf's Up
to buy a new bathing suit.
But there's so much neat stuff
I want to buy the whole store.

I can't believe what they make
with regular old shells:
a pretty music box, a huge shell house,
musical chimes, shiny shell jewelry.

Mom, this horseshoe crab shell
is only $4.99. Can I get it?
"Billy, you can pick them up
off the beach for free."

Look! Bottled sand, bottled seawater,
wooden gulls, painted buoys,
plastic lobsters, big blue fish,
real live snails in saltwater bowls.

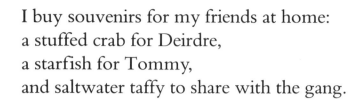

I buy souvenirs for my friends at home:
a stuffed crab for Deirdre,
a starfish for Tommy,
and saltwater taffy to share with the gang.

Mom's calling me across the store.
She's holding up a pair
of glow-in-the-dark jams.
All the surfers wear them.

I pick jams with pockets
reaching down to my knees.
Big boxy jams, pink
with green fishes.

Underwater,
Balloon Fish

"Make a balloon," Nana said.
"Blow your cheeks up real big."

So I did like she said,
put my face in the water
and let the air out slowly.
But bubbles went up my nose.

"Out your nose, too,
like you're blowing into a hanky."

So I did what she said,
put my face in the water,
pretended I had a cold.
But the salt stung my eyes.

"You'll get used to it.
You'll miss too much if you close 'em."

So I kept my eyes open,
and underwater I saw
Nana's red toenails dig in the sand,
little blue fish zigzag away,
crabs crawl sideways under big rocks,
seashells somersault with the waves,

and I saw other balloon fish just like me.

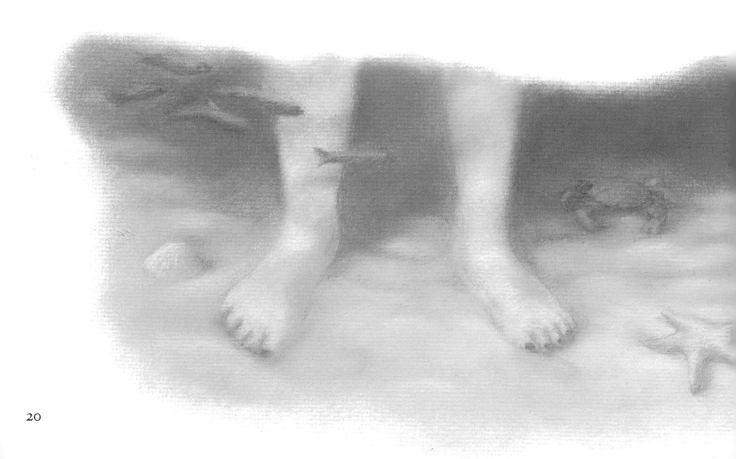

Crabbing

Every year, Pop-Pop takes me
crabbing at the inlet
where he used to take Dad.
He says low tide's the best
because the rocks poke
out of the water,
and we can watch the crabs
crawl under them to hide.
The rocks are all wet
and slippery. We wear sneakers
so the crabs don't pinch us.

Pop-Pop ties a snail onto my line,
and we find a good spot
where the water comes up to my knees.
The waves make the snail move
back and forth like it's alive.

Hey!
"Pull 'em up,"
Pop-Pop yells.
I yank the string
but the crab falls off.

"I lost many a blue devil
that way when I was your age.
Bring 'em up slower next time."

These crabs are so dumb,
they keep coming back.
Take it, take it,
nicely, nicely,
up
and
into the bucket!

"And he didn't even eat your bait."

Me and Pop-Pop have a race
to see who can catch the most crabs
before the water covers the rocks again.
Pop-Pop wins by eight crabs.
"I've been crabbin' this joint
for over fifty years."
I come in second with ten crabs.
"I'm hungry as a shark."

Me, too. So we pack up the big ones
to take home to boil and eat
with melted butter,
but we throw the little ones back.

See you next year, crabbies!

Boogie Boys

Boogie boys surf where it's deep,
standing up or lying down, spinning
and flipping on the waves rolling in.

Jackie next door is a boogie boy.
He wears long flowery jams
or tight black pants.

He has a beezer haircut, muscles
and a tan. He has friends
who ride boogie boards, too.

Jackie has a little sister, Sarah,
who surfs on a skimmer board.
They call her Boogie-ette.

"Can you ride a skateboard?" she asks me.
Sure, can't everyone?
"Well, watch this," she says.

And she throws her round board
like a Frisbee—but not in the air,
on the sand where the waves wash in.

Then she runs and jumps on the board
and sails on the inch of water,
till the next wave crashes down.

"I shot the pipeline on that one,"
she says. "Wanna try, Billy? It's easy.
Like skateboarding, but on the water."

And she throws the board, and I run
and jump…and watch
the board sail off by itself.

"Here, try again." She throws it
and I'm off. I jump,
I hit it! But I fall on my butt.

All the boogie boys stop to watch.
"Third time's the trick, Billy," Jackie says.
And there goes the skimmer!

I run as fast as I can, jump, and
I'm on it, I'm on it,
I'm still on it!

Then crash, a wave. I'm off it.
Sand stings the palms of my hands.
Ugh, a noseful. Oh, don't cry now.

"Billy, that was great!" Sarah says
as she wipes sand off my back.
"Except for one thing." Yeah?

"Now that you're a boogie junior,
you'll have to get a beezer, dude."

Surf Casting

Dad wakes me up
when it's still dark out.
We eat cereal in the kitchen
and don't make a sound.

He grabs the long poles
and I get the bucket.
At the beach it's so foggy
you can't see the water.

I watch him put skinny fish
on the ends of the lines.
Then he shows me how
to open the reel

and hold the line
with my finger.
Then, looking both ways
to make sure the coast is clear,

I turn and bend backwards,
lay my pole back straight,
then hold tight, whip it
forward, and watch the bait fly.

Dad tells me the Indians
used to take the trails
through the Pines every summer
to fish in the ocean.

I'm going to catch fish
the way the Indians did.
I'll catch enough to feed
the whole tribe of Tooles.

We don't talk much more.
We just stand and cast.
Even when the sun comes up,
we just stand and cast.

Bluefish Forever

Dad and I catch five bluefish
this morning, but we only keep three,
just enough for us for dinner.

"The Lenape Indians believed
you should take from the earth
only what you need," Daddy says.

That way there will be plenty
for everyone, even the big fish
who have to eat, too, I say.

"That's right. You know,
if we don't play by the earth's rules,
she's not going to play at all."

You mean, she won't give us crabs
and clams and fish anymore?
"It's possible, son."

At night, I watch Dad squeeze limes
on the fish and cook them on the grill.
When we eat, I chew slowly.

I want to eat bluefish forever.

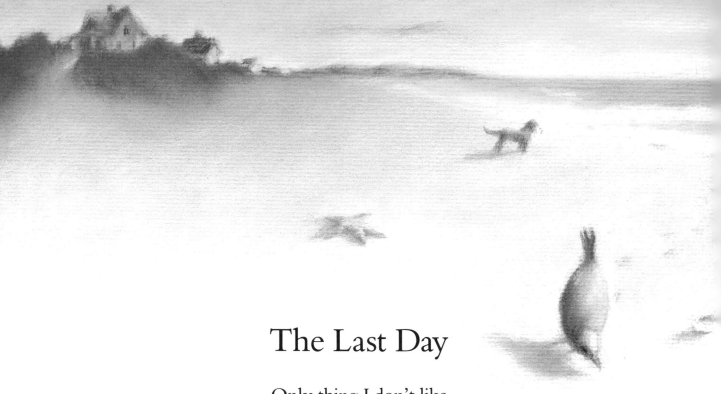

The Last Day

Only thing I don't like
about the beach
is leaving it.

On the day we go home,
I'm the first one up.
I pull on my shorts

and walk down to the beach.
No one is awake but me
and the gulls and terns—

their tracks are everywhere
on the hard wet sand.
I follow them awhile

and make my own tracks.
But I know the tide
will wash them away.

I need something to take
with me. Not just a shell,
something that will keep

the smell of the sea
all year. Driftwood!
Yes, and seaweed, sca tinsel.

I sit down and dig my tocs
into the sand, say good-bye
to ticklish sandcrabs.

I stay and watch the sun
come up over the water
inch by inch.

When it's a big red ball
and the sea is pink,
it's time to go.

Going Home

The car seems smaller,
there's so much stuff.
I can see Nana and Pop-Pop

in between my new skimmer board
and the suitcases, waving
good-bye as we pull away.

Everyone's driving home
in the same direction.
Doesn't anybody live *here*?

The cars on the highway
seem chained to each other
like beads on a necklace.

Dad yells at the traffic,
and Mom complains about
the sand in the car.

But the traffic just gives me
more time to smell the sea.
And I know the sand,

crunching between my toes,
will still shake in my sneakers
in the middle of winter.